TALES FROM THE
BROTHERS GRIMM

Tales from the
Brothers Grimm

A Classic Illustrated Edition

Compiled by Cooper Edens

chronicle books · san francisco

Here's to the Brothers Grimm,
and to all their friends and next-door neighbors —C. E.

Book design by Susan Van Horn.
Typeset in Granjon and Serlio.
Manufactured in China.

Library of Congress Cataloging-in-Publication Data
Edens, Cooper.
Tales from the Brothers Grimm: a classic illustrated edition / [written and] compiled by Cooper Edens.
p. cm.
Summary: Fifteen classic Grimm fairy tales, illustrated by such well-known artists as
Arthur Rackham, Walter Crane, and Randolph Caldecott.
ISBN-13: 978-0-8118-5459-7
ISBN-10: 0-8118-5459-0
1. Fairy tales—Germany. [1. Fairy tales. 2. Folklore—Germany.] I. Grimm, Jacob, 1785–1863.
II. Grimm, Wilhelm, 1786–1859. III. Title.
PZ8.E18Tal 2007
[398.2]—dc22
2006026382

Distributed in Canada by Raincoast Books
9050 Shaughnessy Street, Vancouver, British Columbia V6P 6E5

10 9 8 7 6 5 4 3 2 1

Chronicle Books LLC
680 Second Street, San Francisco, California 94107

www.chroniclekids.com

PREFACE

A LONG TIME AGO, THERE WERE TWO BROTHERS WHO set off to explore the world.

These brothers were professors, and they hoped in their travels to study the way people spoke in different parts of the land. When they met people along the way, the brothers would ask them to tell their favorite stories, and the brothers listened carefully. The brothers heard many, many tales—some long, some short. There were stories about princesses and soldiers, fairies and fishermen. Some were magical, some were adventurous, and some were funny.

Eventually the brothers felt they had gathered enough stories for their studies, and decided their travels were done. But journeys have a way of changing things. When the brothers returned, they were no longer just professors. They had become storytellers.

It is now nearly two hundred years since the Brothers Grimm wrote these stories down. The stories themselves have been on a journey through the years, and have changed a bit, too. The ones included here are retellings in the popular tradition.

No one knows how long these stories had been around before the brothers wrote them down, but stories have a way of living for a very long time. A good story, in fact, may live forever.

—*Cooper Edens*

TABLE OF CONTENTS

CINDERELLA

ONCE UPON A TIME THERE WAS A GIRL NAMED
Isabella whose mother had died, and whose father had remarried. The stepmother brought her two daughters from a previous marriage, and all three of
them were by nature proud, vain, and selfish.

They were never kind to Isabella, but when her father died and they were
left in charge of the household, they felt they could finally treat Isabella just as
they liked, and they were very cruel to her indeed.

They took her room from her, and her fine clothes, and sent her to work
in the kitchen with the servants. Without a bed to sleep in, Isabella had no
choice but to curl up on the hearth by the fire, for the nights were very cold
and she had just a scrap of blanket.

So her plain dress was often dirty from the cinders, and her stepsisters
laughed at her and changed her name to Cinderella.

Poor Isabella worked hard with the servants all day long and slept on the
hard hearthstone every night. But she said her prayers, and bore her punish-
ments patiently.

Then one day, a messenger came to the house with an invitation from the
king: a royal ball would be held, to last two nights, and all the young ladies of
good family in the kingdom were invited, for at this ball the prince would
choose a bride.

The invitation was for Isabella and her stepsisters, but no one said anything about Isabella going. "Cinderella!" they cried. "Lay out our ball gowns and draw us a bath! Then you can curl our hair, and get the carriage ready."

Isabella patiently waited on them, and when she was done, she went to her stepmother and said bravely, "The invitation was for me, also. What dress shall I wear?"

Her stepmother laughed in her face. "There's no dress for you! Go back and sit in the cinders, where you belong. You're no daughter of mine!"

Isabella ran back to the kitchen and sat down by the fire and wept. Her stepmother and stepsisters left for the ball, and night slowly fell around Isabella as the embers went out, one by one.

Suddenly bright flames leaped up before Isabella, filling the fireplace with gold and white. And there, standing in the sparkling fire, stood a beautiful lady. "There now, what's all this?" she asked.

"Oh!" gasped Isabella. "Who are you?"

"Why, your fairy godmother, of course," said the lady. "Your mother asked me to watch over you. You're a good girl, and you have a strong spirit. So no more tears. It's time to go to the ball."

Isabella stood there in shock. "But I can't go to the ball," she said.

"Don't be silly. You can if you have a coach," said the fairy. "Let me see. Run and check the mousetrap and bring back any mice you find, and catch the three green lizards that live behind the waterspout. And then bring me a pumpkin from the garden."

Isabella didn't know what to think of all this, but she ran and did as the fairy asked. In the mousetrap she found six mice, and she caught the sleepy lizards from behind the waterspout. In the garden she found a great golden pumpkin, and she rolled it to the kitchen where the fairy stood.

"Thank you, dear," said the fairy, and she waved her magic wand. In a twinkling, the mice became six little white horses, and the pumpkin a little golden coach, and the lizards a little driver and footmen in neat green uniforms. They rolled out of the kitchen to the dooryard and grew, and grew, until all were full-sized.

The fairy looked very pleased with herself. "Perfect!" she declared. "Now off you go!"

"But," said Isabella sadly, looking down at her dirty dress.

"Oh, of course!" exclaimed the fairy. She waved her magic wand again, and there where Isabella's dress had been was a dress as golden and shining as flame.

"Is that everything?" asked the fairy, tapping her chin and looking Isabella up and down. "Oh, dear!" she cried, looking at Isabella's bare feet. "How could I forget?" She waved her wand one last time, and on Isabella's feet were two sparkling glass slippers.

"Now off you go!" cried the fairy, hurrying Isabella into the coach even as Isabella tried to thank her. "And remember—this magic will last just until midnight. When the day ends, so must all this. Remember!" And away rolled the coach to the palace before Isabella had time to think.

When Isabella walked into the palace's ballroom, there was a sudden hush and everyone turned to stare at the beautiful young woman.

Isabella was so happy to be there that she glowed, and the prince walked up to her as if in a dream, and asked her to dance. One dance after another, after another, and the prince would dance with no one else. Everyone wondered who the lovely girl could be, and even Isabella's own stepmother and stepsisters did not recognize her.

Isabella and the prince only had eyes for each other, and before either realized it, hours had passed. Above the ballroom, the great clock struck half past eleven.

Isabella gave a start of surprise and rushed from the ballroom, leaving the prince bewildered. Out of the palace and down the front stairs and into her coach she ran, and the coach swept her away from the palace and down the long road home. It arrived in Isabella's courtyard just as the clock struck twelve.

Isabella danced into the kitchen and thanked her fairy godmother copiously.

"You're welcome, dear," replied the fairy. "I'll be watching over you. If you need anything else, go to the hazel tree in the garden and wish. I'll hear you." And in a flash of light, she was gone.

On the second night of the ball, Isabella helped her sisters into their dresses and brushed their hair. The sisters, of course, only complained: about their dresses, and about the mysterious princess who had taken up so much of the prince's time the night before; about their hair, and about the princess; about their ribbons, and about the princess.

"I should like to see this princess," said Isabella. "Wouldn't you lend me one of your gowns so that I could go to the ball?"

"Ugh!" cried the sisters. "You? You'd get our dresses all filthy. And the ball is for ladies, not kitchen maids!" And they strutted off to the ball like peacocks.

Cinderella

But once they had gone, Isabella ran to the garden and knelt by the hazel tree. "Fairy godmother, hear me, please," she whispered. And she wished to go to the ball once more. There was the sound of wings, and from the tree floated down Isabella's glass slippers and a new dress, as bright as the sparks that flew up the chimney, and twinkling with diamonds. There in the courtyard once again stood the golden coach and its white horses and green-uniformed footmen, and her fairy godmother, waiting for her.

"Remember," said the fairy as she helped Isabella into the coach, "the magic will last only until midnight!"

Isabella hurried off to the ball in her golden carriage, and when she arrived the prince took her hand and would dance with no one else. The time flew by, and suddenly Isabella heard the great clock strike the first, deep note of twelve.

"Oh!" cried Isabella, remembering the fairy's warning. "I must go!" And she dropped the prince's hand and ran from the room.

The prince ran after her, but she dashed down the palace steps like the wind, dropping a single sparkling glass slipper on the stairs. But no sooner had she reached the bottom of the stairs than the last stroke of twelve rang from the palace. The fairy magic guttered out and disappeared: Isabella's coach

became a pumpkin once more, the mice and lizards ran away into the fields, and Isabella ran home in her plain dress, barefoot, with just one sparkling slipper in her hand.

The next day, while her stepsisters were complaining about the mysterious princess again, another messenger arrived from the king. He announced that the prince had chosen his bride, but she had run away before the prince could ask for her hand, and now he had just her slipper with which to find her. So the prince was traveling from one house to the next, trying to find the girl whose foot fit the slipper, and each household should make ready to receive him.

Of course the stepsisters were delighted to have another chance with the prince, and threw themselves into their best dresses. When the prince arrived, they simpered and fawned over him and tried to stuff their ungainly feet into the dainty slipper. But one stepsister's foot was too wide, and the other's was too long, and the prince shook his head and said, "Are there no other ladies in the house?"

"No," replied the stepsisters, "unless you count Cinderella in the kitchen!" And they laughed.

But the prince carried the slipper into the kitchen, and when he saw Isabella there, he saw the lady he had fallen in love with. He knelt in the cinders and put the slipper on Isabella's little foot. It fit perfectly.

So the prince and Isabella were married, and she wore her beautiful slippers on her wedding day.

Her stepsisters, of course, were beside themselves with jealousy, but Isabella told them that they might come to stay at the palace anytime they liked: there would always be a bed ready for them—on the hearthstone, among the cinders.

HANSEL AND GRETEL

ONCE UPON A TIME THERE WAS A POOR WOODCUTTER who lived on the edge of a great forest with his wife and two children. His son he called Hansel, and his daughter he called Gretel. But cutting wood would not earn enough money to feed all four of them, and gradually they had to sell most of their belongings.

The woodcutter's wife, who was a stingy, mean woman, said to her husband one night, "If this goes on much longer, we shall starve to death! There is nothing to do but get rid of the children. Without them, we shall be able to feed ourselves."

The woodcutter didn't like this at all, but his wife's will was iron. "We'll take them into the forest tomorrow," she said, "and leave them." The woodcutter wept, but he was weak, and in the end he agreed.

Hansel and Gretel, however, had been lying awake, and had heard their parents talking. "Don't worry," whispered Hansel. "I'll take a crust of bread with me and drop crumbs to mark the way home."

The next day, the woodcutter and his wife took Hansel and Gretel into the forest. As they walked, Hansel threw down crumbs of bread on the path. Finally they stopped, and the woodcutter told the children to sit down there and wait for him to return. And he and his wife went away through the woods.

Hansel and Gretel waited a little while, and then got up and began to follow the path of crumbs back home. But they had not gone very many steps when they found that the crumbs were gone, eaten by the forest birds. They were frightened, but they kept walking, hoping to find the right path. The woods grew darker and darker, and soon they knew they were lost.

Cold, scared, and hungry, they wandered in the twilight, until on an over-
hanging branch they saw a pretty little bird with a long, bright tail. Without
any other guide, they followed it, but each time they drew close to it, it flew
just a bit farther on. Before they realized it, Hansel and Gretel had followed
the little bird to a dim clearing in the woods, where there stood a little cottage
with dark windows.

Forgetting the bird, they hurried toward the cottage, and when they came up close, they found to their surprise that the house was made of gingerbread and decorated all around with candies and icing.

They were ravenous, and immediately broke off a bit here and there and began eating. But a whispery, raspy voice came from inside the cottage and said,

> *"Who's that nibbling like a mouse?*
> *Who's that nibbling on my house?"*

Out of the door peeked a little old woman with dim little eyes. "Come in, come in, my dears," she said in her hoarse little voice. "You must be very hungry indeed!"

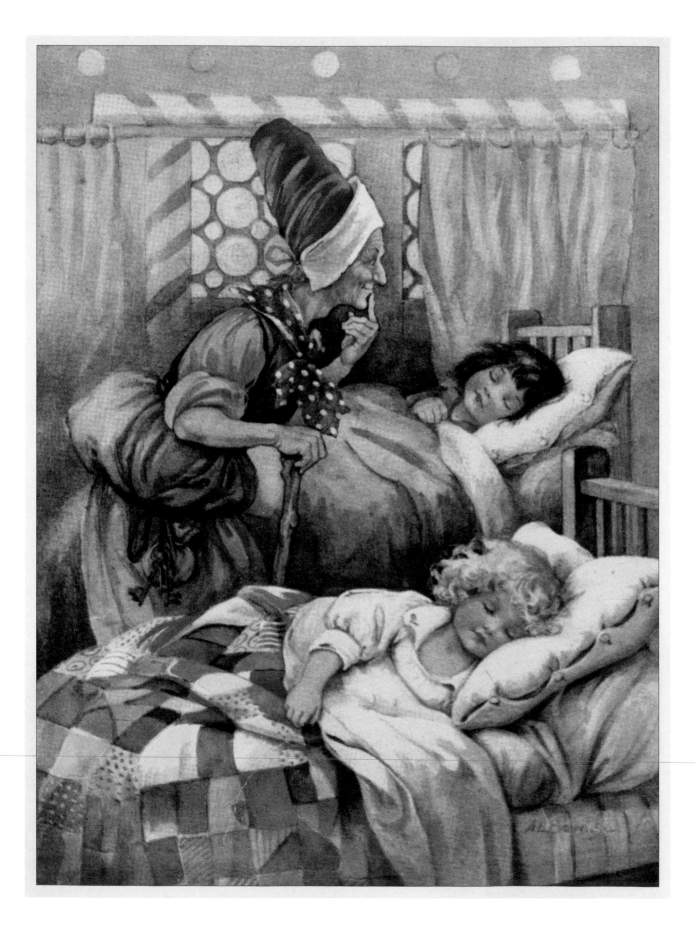

Hansel and Gretel went into the cottage, and there the old woman gave them sweet things to eat and made up two cozy beds for them to sleep in.

But the old woman was a wicked witch, and all the while she was feeding them and tucking them into bed, she was admiring their rosy cheeks and little limbs, and thinking how delicious they would be.

As soon as the children were sleeping soundly, she carried Hansel to a big cage and stuffed him inside, singing to herself,

> *"What do we like best to eat?*
>
> *Little boys, fat and sweet!"*

In the morning, she kicked Gretel awake. "Don't just lie there, you worthless thing!" she cried. "Fetch water from the well and light the fire. There is work to do!"

So Gretel had to work hard every day for the witch, while the witch waited for Hansel to get fat enough to eat. Every day, she went to the cage and said, "Stick your finger through the bars!" But Hansel stuck a stick through the bars instead, and the witch, who was nearly blind, felt the stick and said, "Too thin, too thin!"

So it went for days and days, until the witch was mad with impatience and hunger. "Fine!" she screeched. "If he will not fatten, I'll eat him lean!" And she laid a fire under the great oven and stoked it till it blazed.

When the oven was hot, the witch said to Gretel, "Test the oven, and tell me if it's time to bake."

But Gretel said, "How shall I test it?"

"Silly goose!" said the witch. "Do I have to do everything myself?" And she opened the oven door and leaned in to test the temperature.

Quick as a wink, Gretel pushed the old witch into the oven and shut the door behind her. Then she ran to Hansel's cage and let him out, and together they opened the witch's chests and coffers and found bright jewels and heaps of coins. They filled their pockets and ran away from the cottage through the forest.

Soon they found themselves at the top of a hill, and from there they saw the edge of the woods, and so easily made their way home. Their father was overjoyed to see them safe and whole after all this time, and he hugged them tightly and wept. Gretel shook out her pinafore, and Hansel turned out his pockets, and the twinkling stones and gold coins fell all over the ground.

Their mother, meanwhile, had died, and so Hansel and Gretel and the woodcutter made their home together in happiness. In time, Hansel grew quite big and strong and owned all the woods and fields thereabout; and Gretel became a very fine baker.

Rose Red and
Rose White

Once upon a time there were two sisters named
Rose Red and Rose White. They lived with their mother in a little cottage surrounded by rose bushes, and the bushes bore flowers that twined red and
white all about the house and garden.

Rose Red and Rose White often spent time in the woods, and were such
quiet and gentle girls that the woodland creatures grew to trust them. The
deer would sniff their pockets for apples, and the wild rabbits would eat let-
tuce from their hands.

In the evenings, Rose Red and Rose White sat by the fire with their
mother, reading. But one winter evening, after night had fallen and all was
dark and cold outside the cottage, there came a great knock at the door.

Rose Red went to the door and pushed the bolt back, but when she looked
outside, there on the doorstep was a tall black bear. She cried out, but the bear
spoke and said, "Please don't be frightened. I've heard how kind you are to the
forest animals, and only hoped to warm myself by your fire. I am half-frozen."

"You poor bear," said Rose Red's mother. "Please come in." So the bear laid himself before the fire, and Rose Red and Rose White brushed the snow from his fur and scratched his ears, and the bear sighed in pleasure and soon fell fast asleep.

After that, the bear came to their cottage every evening, and became a good friend to the girls. They would play until bedtime, and then the bear would curl up in front of the hearth until morning.

But when spring came, the bear went away into the forest again. Rose Red and Rose White missed their friend greatly, and hoped to see him when they went walking in the woods. But spring turned into summer, and the bear was not to be found.

Then, one day, as Rose Red and Rose White were out in the woods, they saw a little man jumping about and yelling furiously. He had caught the tip of his long beard in a fallen log and could not get it free.

Rose Red and Rose White ran to help him, but pull as they might, they couldn't get the little man's beard out. So Rose White took her little scissors and cut the bottom of the little man's beard off.

"Oh!" cried the little man in a rage. "How rude! How dare you cut my beard! Oh! What nasty girls you are!" And without even thanking the girls, he snatched up a bag of rubies from the ground and hopped off through the forest, still yelling.

Not long after, Rose Red and Rose White went out into the woods to gather berries, and there, by the stream, was the little man again, jumping about as before, and with his medium-length beard tangled in some fishing line. The other end of the line had been swallowed by a large fish, and the fish was about to pull the little man into the water.

"What are you standing about for?" screamed the little man at them. "Help me, you silly, silly girls!"

So Rose Red and Rose White ran and tried to untangle the fishing line, but found they couldn't, and finally Rose White took out her scissors and cut off some more of the little man's beard.

"Aaa!" cried the little man, turning bright red with anger. "You horrible, horrible girls!" And again, without a word of thanks for Rose Red and Rose White, the little man snatched up a sack of pearls from the ground and rushed away, screaming insults back at them.

Some days later, Rose Red and Rose White were walking through the woods on their way to town, and once again, they saw the little man. This time an eagle had a hold of his short beard, and was trying to carry him away. The little man was shouting for help and swatting desperately at the eagle, so once again Rose Red and Rose White went to help him. They waved branches at the eagle and scared it away, but it tore off the rest of the little man's beard as it went.

"Oh!" cried the little man, turning quite blue. "I'll get you both for this! Horrible children!" And he stepped forward to strike them. But suddenly there was a great roar, and there was the tall black bear.

The bear leaped on the little man, and crushed him beneath his great paws.

Then the tall black bear stood up, and his furry bearskin fell off of him. Underneath, he was a handsome young man.

"Rose Red! Rose White!" he said. "You have saved me! That evil gnome cast a spell on me and changed me into a bear, but all his magic was in his beard, and now, now I am free!"

So Rose Red and Rose White and the young man who had been a bear went home together. They found the gnome's hoard of jewels, and with that wealth they built a cottage for the young man next to the rose cottage, and all around it they planted saxifrage, which is called bear flower. And they all lived happily ever after.

Snow White and the Seven Dwarfs

ONCE UPON A TIME THERE WAS A QUEEN WHO LONGED for a daughter. When the baby came, she was the most beautiful child anyone had ever seen, with lips as red as holly berries, skin as white as snow, and hair as black as earth. The queen loved her fiercely and named her Snow White.

But soon after, the queen fell sick and died, and after some time the king married another woman. She was beautiful and proud, but had a heart like ice.

The new queen had no love for Snow White. She spent most of her time admiring herself in her mirror and asking it questions. It was a magic mirror and would answer any question truthfully, but what the queen asked it most frequently was this:

> "Mirror, mirror, on the wall;
> Who is fairest of us all?"

And the mirror answered her every time,

> "North and south, east and west,
> for beauty only you are best."

But Snow White's beauty grew with each passing year, and one day the
queen stopped before her mirror and asked,

> *"Mirror, mirror, on the wall;*
>
> *Who is fairest of us all?"*

And the mirror replied,

> *"Fair as day after winter's night,*
>
> *Snow White is fairest in my sight."*

The queen turned pale with rage and envy, but the mirror would not change its answer. Jealousy grew in the queen's heart like a storm, until she could not look in any mirror for shame, and she could not stand the sight of Snow White for hatred.

Finally she called the royal huntsman to her. "Take Snow White into the forest," she ordered, "and bring me back her heart."

The huntsman led Snow White away into the forest and pulled out his knife. But his hand trembled and he found he couldn't bear to kill her. He told Snow White what the queen had ordered him to do. "So you must run away," he told her. "Find someplace to hide far away from here!" He was sure she would die in the winter woods, left all alone. He killed a deer, and took its heart back to the queen in place of Snow White's heart.

Snow White wandered through the forest all day, lost and alone, until she was cold and hungry and more tired than she had ever been. And then in a clearing deep in the forest, she found a small cottage.

Inside there was a table with seven plates of food laid out, and seven beds stood along the wall. Snow White ate a little from each plate, drank a little from one of the cups, and then curled up in the farthest bed, and was soon fast asleep.

The owners of the cottage were seven dwarfs who mined the mountain all day, and only came home at night. When they returned to their cottage, they were surprised to find the table was not as they had left it.

"Someone has moved my stool," said the first.

"Someone has eaten off my plate," said the second.

"And someone has taken a bit of my bread," said the third.

"Someone has used my spoon," said the fourth.

"And someone has used my fork," said the fifth.

"Someone has cut with my knife," said the sixth.

"And look," said the seventh, "someone has drunk from my cup."

Then they looked about, and to their great surprise they found Snow White, asleep in one of the beds.

Their voices woke Snow White. But when she had told them her story, they took pity on her and agreed to let her stay if she would keep the house for them. Snow White accepted gladly.

So Snow White came to live with the dwarfs. She cooked and cleaned for them, and made their house a cheerful place. Every morning the dwarfs went into the mountains to cut the rock in search of gold and precious stones, and every evening they came home to a clean house, a good meal, and Snow White's laughter. Soon the dwarfs loved her like a daughter. Days passed into weeks, and Snow White found she was happier there than she had ever been.

But far away in the castle, the queen believed Snow White was dead. Slowly, she was able to forget that her beauty was once second-best, and one day she went again to her mirror and asked it her question:

> *"Mirror, mirror, on the wall;*
>
> *Who is fairest of us all?"*

But the mirror replied,

> *"Though she is hidden, it is true:*
>
> *Snow White is still more fair than you."*

Then the queen knew Snow White was alive, and her hatred flared up even stronger than before. The queen could neither eat nor sleep, and determined to find Snow White and watch her die.

She filled a basket with apples, and on the ripest one she dripped a deadly poison. Then she disguised herself as a poor old woman and set off into the forest.

When she found the dwarfs' cottage, she called up to the window, "Apples! Sweet apples for sale!" She chose one of the unpoisoned apples and took a bite, so that the scent would carry up to the window.

Snow White came to the window and looked out. "They smell lovely," she said, "but I don't have any money to spend. But please come inside and have a cup of tea. You must be tired from walking so far in the forest."

When the queen had drunk her tea, she said to Snow White, "What a good girl you are. For your hospitality, take this apple with my thanks." And she pressed the poisoned apple into Snow White's hand.

Snow White thanked her kindly and took a bite of the rosy fruit. But the bite stuck in Snow White's throat. At once her breath stopped, and she fell down as if dead. The queen was much satisfied, and hurried away back to the castle.

When the dwarfs returned to their cottage that evening, they found Snow White lying as still and cold as death, and wept many tears. But she was still

as lovely as ever, and they could not bear to bury her. So they made her a beautiful glass coffin and set it in the clearing, where they could visit her every day.

There she lay for a long time, until the first flowers bloomed next to her. One day a king came wandering through the forest. He saw Snow White, and loved her immediately. When the dwarfs returned, he begged them to let him take her away with him, and promised to keep her safe. The dwarfs were very reluctant to give her away, but the king was so desperately in love that they took pity on him and agreed.

But no sooner did the king lift her from the coffin than the piece of apple fell out of Snow White's mouth, and she woke from her long sleep. Then the dwarfs wept with joy and embraced her, and the king asked her to come home with him and be his wife.

Snow White agreed, and went away with the king, and they were married in his palace, where they lived and reigned happily for many, many years.

But the evil queen returned to her castle and asked the mirror once more who was the fairest of them all. And the mirror replied,

> *"Lady, you are very fair,*
> *But fairer shines there one.*
> *You are bright as starlight,*
> *But Snow White is the sun."*

Then the queen's withered heart broke within her, and she fell down dead, her skin as pale as snow.

THE CHANGELING

ONCE UPON A TIME THERE WAS A POOR WOMAN who was the mother of a beautiful baby, and that child was all the treasure the woman wanted in the world.

But one morning when the mother went to the crib, instead of her happy, laughing child, she found a horrible changeling child with blank eyes and heavy limbs in her child's place.

She was terrified for her baby and ran out into the road to see if she could tell who had stolen it, but there was no one in the road but an old woman with a cane. The mother sat down and began to cry in despair.

"What's the matter, dear?" asked the old woman, stopping by the gate.

The mother explained what had happened, and the old woman replied, "Your child has been stolen away by the fairies, but perhaps if you can make the changeling child laugh, the fairies will take it back and return your child to you. Go back into your house, turn as many things as you may upside down, boil some water in an eggshell, and wash the changeling well."

The mother was willing to try anything, so she did as the old woman advised. She turned all the things she could upside down, boiled water in an eggshell, and washed the ugly changeling in the water. The changeling child opened its eyes wide, looked about, and began to laugh. Quick as a wink, the hearthstone lifted up, and a fairy man appeared with the human infant. He took up the changeling child and was gone in an instant, and the mother and her child lived happily from that day forth.

THE FROG PRINCE

ONCE UPON A TIME THERE WAS A PRINCESS WHO had a golden ball that she loved better than anything else, and one day, sitting in the garden on the edge of a wide well, she accidentally dropped the ball into the water. It disappeared immediately into the depths, and the princess began to cry.

"Highness, why are you crying?" asked a voice, and there at the edge of the well was a frog, looking at her.

The princess jumped up in disgust, but the frog only looked at her. The princess hesitated a moment. "I dropped my golden ball into the well," she said at last.

"I could get it for you," said the frog, "but if I do, what will you give me in return?"

"I have this pearl necklace," she replied, "or this little gold ring."

"I have no use for jewels," replied the frog, "but if you'll promise to take me up to the palace, and let me eat dinner off of your own plate, and let me sleep on your pillow beside you, I will find you your ball."

The princess did not like this, but she doubted that the frog could do much about it if she broke her promise. So she said, "All right," and the frog dove deep into the water and was gone a long time.

Finally he returned, with the princess's golden ball in his mouth, and the princess took it from him and ran back to the palace, intending to forget about the frog entirely.

That evening the princess was sitting at the dinner table when in hopped the frog. "Who let that frog in?" demanded the king.

But the frog spoke and said, "The princess gave me her word that she would let me eat dinner off of her own plate, and let me sleep on her pillow beside her, if I would find her golden ball." And the king said, "Is this true?"

The princess admitted that it was, and the king replied, "A promise is a promise, and what you have said, you must do." And so the frog hopped up on the table and ate from the princess's plate until he was full.

When it was time for bed, the princess ran up to her room, but the frog hopped slowly after her, and when he reached her room, he said, "Pick me up now, and let me sleep on your pillow!"

The princess was so revolted, however, that instead she picked the frog up and threw him at the wall. Splat! But there, where the frog had been, suddenly in his place was a handsome prince.

"Thank you, Princess," the prince said, and his voice was the voice of the frog. "I have been under an evil enchantment, and you have freed me."

So the prince came to live at the palace, and soon after the princess promised him her heart.

And that promise she kept very well.

LITTLE RED RIDING HOOD

ONCE UPON A TIME THERE WAS A LITTLE GIRL WHO lived on the edge of a dark, dark forest. This little girl often wore a pretty red cape with a hood, and so people called her Little Red Riding Hood.

One morning, Little Red Riding Hood's mother said to her, "Sweetheart, I've packed a basket with some cookies and a pot of soup. Would you take them to your grandmother on the other side of the forest? She's been feeling a little sick."

So Little Red Riding Hood took the basket and started down the path through the forest.

"Don't dawdle," called her mother from the door. "And don't talk to strangers!"

But Little Red Riding Hood forgot her mother's warnings almost immediately. In the forest were some very pretty flowers, and Little Red Riding Hood stopped to pick some for her grandmamma.

Suddenly there in front of her was a great big wolf.

"Hello," said the wolf. "What's a sweet little girl like you doing in the forest?"

"I'm going to my grandmamma's house," said Little Red Riding Hood. "She's sick."

"How sweet," said the wolf. But to himself, he thought, "What a sweet morsel. But the girl's just enough for dessert. I'll have her granny for dinner, and save the little girl for after."

So the wolf wished Little Red Riding Hood a pleasant walk and ran off through the forest to her grandmother's house. Little Red Riding Hood picked some more flowers and daydreamed down the path, not hurrying.

When the wolf came to the cottage of Little Red Riding Hood's grandmother, he knocked on the door and said in a high, sweet voice, "Grandmamma, it's me, Little Red Riding Hood. I have some goodies for you."

"Come in, darling," said Little Red Riding Hood's grandmother. "The door's unlocked."

The wolf pushed the door in, leaped on Little Red Riding Hood's grandmother, and swallowed her in an instant. Then he put on her nightgown and her nightcap, and lay down in her bed with the lights off and the covers pulled all the way up.

In a little while, Little Red Riding Hood arrived at the cottage and knocked on the door.

"Grammy?" she called. "It's me."

"Come in, darling," called the wolf in a little old lady voice. "I'm here in bed."

Little Red Riding Hood came into the cottage and went to her grandmother's bedroom door. "I brought you some cookies and soup from Mommy," she said in the darkened room.

"That's nice, dear," said the wolf. "Come to the bed, where I can see you."

Little Red Riding Hood went to the bed, where she was very much astonished to see how her grandmother looked in her nightclothes. "Grammy," she said, "what a big nose you have!"

"The better to smell the yummy things to eat," said the wolf, and his mouth was watering.

Little Red Riding Hood stepped a little closer. "Grammy," she said, "what big eyes you have!"

"The better to see you with, darling," said the wolf softly.

Little Red Riding Hood moved a little closer. "Grammy," she whispered, "what big teeth you have!"

"The better to eat you up with!" the wolf roared, and gulped Little Red Riding Hood whole. Then he lay back down, patted his very full stomach, and went to sleep.

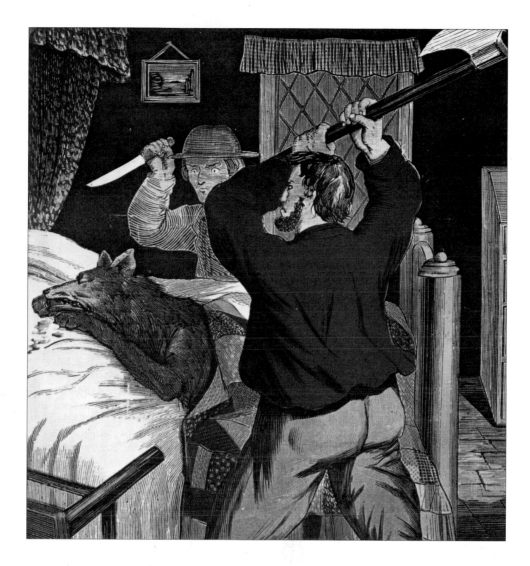

But two passing woodsmen had heard the wolf's roar, and hurried up to the cottage. When they saw the wolf asleep in the old lady's bed with a big, fat stomach, they guessed what had happened. With ax and knife, they cut the wolf's stomach open and out hopped Little Red Riding Hood and her grandmother, whole and well, but very frightened. They thanked the woodsmen again and again.

Together they tidied the cottage, and the woodsmen went away with the wolf slung between them. Little Red Riding Hood tucked her grandmother back in bed, and gave her her cookies and soup. And then Little Red Riding Hood walked home again, and she did not stop along the way.

SLEEPING BEAUTY

ONCE UPON A TIME THERE WAS A CASTLE SURROUNDED by roses that were known far and wide for the beauty and fragrance of their blooms. The king and queen who lived there loved and nurtured the roses, and when they had a baby daughter, they named her Briar Rose.

To celebrate the princess's birth, the king and queen held a great feast and invited the fairies of the land to be godmothers to the little girl. The king and queen had only twelve golden plates, and so they invited only twelve fairies.

But there were thirteen fairies in the kingdom, and the thirteenth, rarely seen and much disliked, found out that she had been excluded, crept out of her wild woods, and followed the road to the castle.

When the feast concluded, the twelve fairies stood up from their places and came one by one to kiss the princess and give her their gifts. One fairy gave her kindness, and another gave her grace; one gave her generosity, and another fairness. Health, humor, intelligence, wit, patience, beauty, courage . . . and the twelfth fairy was just about to give her gift when, with a horrible screech, the thirteenth fairy threw open the doors.

"I was not invited,"
she hissed, and her voice seemed
to slither among the guests. "But
even so, I have something special for
the princess. My gift is this: You shall
have her for a while, but when she
comes of age, Briar Rose will prick her finger on a spinning wheel's spindle, and she
will fall down dead!"

A gust of wind whipped through the room, and
the evil fairy was gone. The king and queen cried out
in horror and despair, but the twelfth fairy, who had
not yet given her gift, stepped forward and spoke.

"I cannot undo what has been done," she said,
"but perhaps I can change the curse somewhat. Briar
Rose shall prick her finger, but when she does she
will fall not into death, but into a great sleep. A hundred years she'll dream away, till someone comes
bearing the gift I could not give her today."

The king and queen ordered all the spinning wheels in the kingdom burned, and outlawed the making of new ones. The years passed, and
gradually their fears gave way to time, and they began to hope that nothing
would come of the evil fairy's curse.

But Briar Rose grew up just as the fairies had foretold, wise and just and
giving, beautiful and kind. Everyone adored her, but on her sixteenth birthday, when all the castle was preparing for her birthday celebration, she was
left alone. Wandering the castle, Briar Rose found a narrow staircase in a

tower she had not seen before, and when she reached the top, there in a tiny room was an old woman spinning wool into yarn on a spinning wheel.

"Happy birthday," said the old woman in a soft voice that seemed to wrap itself around the princess.

"Hello," said Briar Rose, stepping closer. "What are you doing there?"

"Spinning, of course," whispered the old woman. "Why, haven't you seen wool spun into yarn before?" Her eyes glittered. "It's easy. Try it for yourself."

Briar Rose reached out her hand, and no sooner had she touched the sharpened spindle than she pricked her finger, and fell down as though dead. The old woman laughed a bitter laugh and disappeared out the window.

When Briar Rose was found beside the spinning wheel, the King and Queen were much grieved. They had her carried to her bed, and sat by her all day, hoping still that she might wake.

At sunset, the twelfth good fairy returned to the castle. She looked closely at Briar Rose. "The princess is sleeping, as I promised," she told the King and Queen. "And now you must sleep as well, until time can soften the curse, and someone comes who may break it."

She waved her wand. Quick as night in winter, sleep fell over all the castle: the king and queen and their court, the cooks and butlers and maids. The horses slept in the stables, and even the fires slept in their hearths.

The roses all around the castle grew up suddenly into a tall forest of deadly spikes, through which even the castle's high towers could not be seen.

Days grew into months, months grew into years, and years grew into decades. Time passed, until the castle became more legend than truth; until there were people who lived right next to the forest of thorns who were not sure what lay within it.

But finally, after many years, there came a young man to the town at the edge of the forest. He had a brave heart and liked stories, and when he heard the story of the enchanted castle and the sleeping princess, he decided to travel into the forest and see what he would find there.

No one had been able to venture into the forest for a hundred years. The roses were fierce with their thorns, and tore anyone who came near them. But now the young man stepped into the forest, and he found to his wonderment that the roses drew back before him. Where he passed, they shed their thorns, and in his wake new flowers opened, until the forest was full of blossoms.

Hurrying along the corridor

When he came to the castle, all was just as it had been at the moment Briar
Rose fell asleep, as still and silent as a held breath. He passed through hall after
hall, and climbed stair after stair, until at last he came to a chamber where a
beautiful girl lay in a golden bed.

He looked at her and lost his heart in an instant. He knelt down beside her and gave her a kiss.

And Briar Rose opened her eyes. Just like that, the spell was broken.

All the castle came alive at once: the king and queen awoke in their throne room, and the court and all the servants shook themselves awake; the horses woke up in the stables, and the fires roared to life in their hearths. And Briar Rose came down to the throne room holding the hand of the young man she loved.

So her birthday celebration became a wedding feast, and all the country for miles around bloomed with the scent of roses.

THE ELVES AND THE SHOEMAKER

ONCE UPON A TIME THERE WAS A POOR SHOEMAKER who had just enough leather left in his shop to make one more pair of shoes. Business had not been good, and he worried that if he did not sell those shoes, he and his wife would surely starve.

"I shall make the finest pair of shoes I can," he thought, "and I shall start first thing in the morning, when the light is best." So he set out the leather and his tools, and went to bed.

But when he came downstairs the next morning, he had a great surprise: there, where the leather had been, were two of the prettiest shoes he'd ever seen, and much better than he could have made them. When he looked, he found the stitches in them were so small they were hard to see, and perfectly straight and even.

The shoemaker couldn't guess who could have made the shoes, but he set them out for sale, and sold them almost immediately. He was able to charge enough for the shoes so that with the money he bought enough leather for three more pairs, and a good dinner for himself and his wife.

As before, he set out the leather that evening and went to bed.

The next morning he found that again the leather had been worked into shoes: three delightful pairs sat on his workbench as though whoever had made them had only just left.

So the shoemaker sold the shoes and bought more leather. And once again he found the leather mysteriously worked into shoes while he slept.

This went on for many days, and soon the shoemaker and his wife had more money than they knew what to do with. They were very grateful to whoever was making the shoes for them, but didn't know how to thank the mysterious person.

"I think we should pretend to go to bed, but stay up and see if we can catch him," said the shoemaker's wife.

"Are you sure?" asked the shoemaker. "He must not want to be caught, coming in the night as he does. Perhaps he wouldn't want us to."

"But we can't go on like this," countered his wife, "owing so much to some-one and not even trying to repay him!"

So they agreed to stay up together, and see if they could discover the myste-rious helper. They sat very quietly on the stairs for hours, and then, at the stroke of midnight, they saw a tiny light come into the workshop.

They peeked around the corner, and what did they see? Three little elves were at the workbench, cutting the leather and sewing and hammering, and working away with their clever little hands. In the twinkling of an eye, the work was done, and more beautiful shoes sat on the workbench, ready to be worn. The work done, the elves vanished.

"My goodness!" exclaimed the shoemaker. "Elves, all this time! Who would have thought?"

"But did you see the little sweethearts?" said his wife. "They had no clothes—just rags! And the night's so cold."

"Well," said the shoemaker, "I don't think elves have any use for money. But perhaps they'd like it if we made them some clothes. At least it would show we're grateful."

So the next day the shoemaker and his wife bought some fine, warm fabrics and sat all day, stitching little pants and shirts and warm jackets for the elves, and the shoemaker, using his smallest needle and his thinnest leather, made two pairs of very, very small, elf-sized shoes. Then they laid all the clothes out on the workbench and went to hide on the staircase again.

Once again, the tiny light appeared at midnight, and the three elves came into the workshop. But how surprised they were to find little clothes, just their size, where usually they found shoe leather! The elves were delighted, and quickly took off their rags and put on their fine new clothes and shoes, with many exclamations of pleasure. Then they vanished as quickly as they'd come.

The shoemaker and his wife never saw the elves again. The money they had made allowed them to live very comfortably for the rest of their lives, and their shoe shop did very well from then on. But they never forgot the help they had received, and the shoemaker always kept a tiny pair of shoes ready on his workbench, just in case.

THE BRAVE
LITTLE TAILOR

ONCE UPON A TIME THERE WAS A TAILOR WHO WAS better at embroidering upon a story than stitching a straight seam. Thus he was very poor, and now there was nothing left to eat in all his house but a crust of bread, a bit of jam, and a lump of old cheese, and no one to share them with but the songbird he kept in a cage.

Having nothing else for breakfast, the tailor spread the jam on the crust of bread, but no sooner had he done this than a crowd of flies swarmed over the jam. "Ruin my breakfast, will you?" he shouted at the flies, and smacked them with a cloth. He looked, and he found he'd killed seven flies at once! Well, he was so proud of himself, that he sat down and made himself a wide belt, and in big fancy letters he stitched across it, "Seven At One Blow!"

Once he had put his belt on and admired himself in it, he decided he was too fine and brave a man to continue being a poor tailor, so he put the lump of cheese in one pocket, and his songbird in another pocket, and set off down the road.

It was not long before he was completely lost. He paid no attention to the path, and soon he was deep in the forest with no idea where to go. Night was falling, so he took shelter in a wide cave.

But it was a giant's cave, and the tailor was just settling down when a big voice came rumbling like thunder from deep inside. "Who's there in my front room?" boomed the voice.

"It's me!" said the tailor, bold as brass. "And you can call me Seven At One Blow!"

The giant came out and looked at the tailor. "Seven At One Blow, ay?" he thundered. "You must think you're very strong."

"Oh, yes," said the tailor. "Much stronger than a weakling like you. Why, I could crush you with one hand! But you seem all right, so let's be friends."

"Hmm," said the giant suspiciously. "If we're friends, then sit down and have a drink of water with me. I like the water squeezed from stones best." And he picked up a stone and squeezed it so tightly in his fist that it sweated drops of water.

"That's my favorite as well!" said the tailor, and he took the lump of cheese from his pocket, held it up, and squeezed it until the water ran out.

"Hmm," said the giant. "You do seem very strong. But I can throw a stone so high it will come down on the other side of the hill. What about you?"

"That's nothing," said the tailor. "I can throw a stone so high that it won't come down at all!" And he took the bird from his pocket and threw it up into the air. The bird flew away into the sky until it could not be seen in the twilight.

Now the giant was worried. He didn't like to have anyone as strong as this Seven At One Blow fellow hanging about. What if he decided he wanted all the gold the giant had stolen?

The giant thought hard. "Well, I'm tired," he said to the tailor, "but as you're my guest, I insist you sleep in my bed tonight." And he lay down on the floor of the cave and soon began to snore.

The tailor cheerfully climbed into the giant's bed, but found it uncomfortable (and smelly). So he climbed out of the bed and curled up on a blanket at the mouth of the cave, where the air was fresh.

Deep in the night, the giant woke and carefully snuck up on the bed where he thought the tailor was sleeping. Then, swinging his great club, he bashed and smashed the bed until he had crushed it into kindling.

The next morning, the giant emerged from the cave, and there, sitting on a stone and admiring the day, was the tailor, looking well rested.

Well, that was enough for the giant. He ran off over the hill and through the forest, and left his gold for the tailor. He didn't want to find out what Seven At One Blow might do next.

The tailor filled his purse with the giant's gold, and wandered on. He walked all day and into the night, until he came out of the forest and found himself before a mighty palace. So he sat down by the gate, and fell asleep.

In the morning, the castle folk found him sleeping there, and ran and told the king about the stranger who had such a full purse and a belt that said Seven At One Blow.

"Hmm," thought the king. "This must be a wandering hero!" And he called the tailor before him.

"I have heard that you're very strong," began the king. (The tailor nodded happily.) "And I have a particular problem. In my kingdom are two giants—brothers who fight with each other all the time and cause much harm. If you'll try to get rid of them, I'll send a hundred horsemen with you."

"No need, no need!" said the tailor cheerfully. "I got rid of one giant all by myself just yesterday! Just point me which way to find them."

The king could not quite believe his ears, but he showed the tailor which road would take him to the giants, and the tailor set off with a merry step.

The tailor walked all morning, down the road and into a deep wood. Just about noon, he heard a rumbling coming from the woods off the road. "That sounds like giant snoring," he thought to himself, and indeed, when he had walked a little way in the direction of the noise, he found the two giants stretched out on the ground, having their afternoon nap.

"Lazy," commented the tailor, and he filled his pockets with stones and climbed a nearby tree.

When he was hidden in the leaves, he threw a stone at one of the giants, and caught him a painful blow on the ear.

"Ouch!" cried the giant, waking up. "What did you do that for?"

"What are you complaining about?" grumbled his brother, rolling over. "Go back to sleep!"

But the tailor threw another stone at the second giant, and got him right on the nose.

"Oh!" yelled the second giant, sitting up. "What's wrong with you, hitting me while I'm sleeping?"

"What's wrong with *you*?" cried the first. "*You* hit *me*, not the other way around!"

"I'll teach you to bash me like a coward and then lie about it!" shouted the second, and soon they were hitting each other in earnest, while the tailor

helped by throwing stones whenever one of the giants turned his back. The two giants were soon so angry that they each yanked up a tree and beat each other viciously until they both fell down, stone dead.

The tailor leaped lightly down from his tree and walked on back to the castle, where he presented himself to the king.

The king had never thought to see Seven At One Blow again, but here he was, claiming to have uprooted two trees and killed both giants. The king sent a man on horseback to confirm what the tailor said, and when he returned with the news that the giants were indeed no more, the king gladly rewarded Seven At One Blow with a hundred purses of gold.

"Listen," said the king to the tailor. "There is a unicorn that lives in the forest. If you can catch it without hurting it, I'll give you a *thousand* purses of gold and the hand of my daughter in marriage!"

The tailor was certain by now that he could do anything, and happily agreed. He took some rope and an ax and went off into the forest. He hadn't gone far when he felt he needed a rest, and leaned against a tree for a breath. But just then the unicorn trotted into view, and, seeing the tailor, lowered its horn and charged. The tailor was so surprised he did not know what to do, and, stumbling to get away, he tripped on a root and fell down just as the unicorn speared the tree where the tailor had stood. The unicorn had run into the tree so hard that its horn was now stuck, and the tailor jumped to his feet and threw the rope around the unicorn's neck.

Once captured, the unicorn became quite tame, and the tailor cut its horn free and led it proudly back to the king. He told a wonderful story about how he had tracked the unicorn down and fought it into submission, and the king was happy to believe him.

The very next day, the tailor was given a thousand purses of gold and married to the princess. The king made him a prince and gave him a fine house to live in. The tailor felt this was an admirable arrangement, and he lived very happily with the princess from that day forth. He gave up being a tailor, and instead he took up storytelling.

The Twelve Dancing Princesses

NCE UPON A TIME THERE WAS A KING WHO HAD twelve beautiful daughters. They slept in a single room of the palace, in twelve silvery beds. There was only one door into this room, and every night there was a guard outside the door.

Yet the king had a problem, for every morning the princesses' dancing slippers were worn through as though the princesses had been dancing all night. Each princess said that she did not know how it happened, but certainly there had to be some magic about it, and this frightened the king. The king's counselors examined the princesses' slippers, and the king's doctors examined the princesses' feet, but no one, finally, could discover the cause. Soon all the country knew that the princesses were bewitched.

In his fear, the king had it proclaimed far and wide that whoever could solve the mystery might claim one of the princesses for his bride . . . but that anyone who tried and failed must be put to death.

One prince after another came to face the challenge. Each was given three days and three nights to find a solution, but one after another lost his head. Soon no one was left who would attempt to solve the puzzle.

Now it happened that a poor soldier passed through the kingdom, and heard of the princesses' bewitchment and the king's challenge.

"I have little enough to lose," he thought, and so he presented himself at the palace and was led before the king.

"You know that many have tried and failed before you?" asked the king.

"I do," said the soldier, "but I will attempt it."

"Then you have three days and three nights, and if you do not have the answer on the morning following, you will die," replied the king.

The soldier was given fine clothes to wear, and fine food to eat, and a fine bed to sleep in. But that night he did not go to bed, but took the guard's place outside the princesses' door.

On the first stroke of midnight, he heard a faint sound from inside the princesses' room, and, peeking inside, was just in time to see the princesses slipping down a long staircase that had opened in the floor. Quickly the soldier followed them, careful not to make a sound.

The stairs went down so far that the soldier was certain they must be underground, but when he reached the bottom of the staircase, he found himself at the edge of a wide lake. Twelve princes waited there, and twelve boats, but when the princes stepped forward to lead the princesses aboard, the soldier took the hand of the youngest princess, and rowed her across.

Across the wide lake was another castle, and alighting there, they entered a wide garden, surrounded by trees whose leaves were silver, whose fruit was gold, and whose flowers sparkled like diamonds.

Sweet music played, and the princes (and the soldier pretending to be one) led the princesses into the dance. They danced under the bright trees for what seemed like hours, until the princesses' slippers were quite worn through, and the music stopped. Then the princesses ran to the boats, and the soldier quickly plucked a silver leaf from one of the trees and followed them. They landed by the stairs and the soldier followed the princesses quickly up to their bedroom, and he reached the top just as the clock chimed the last stroke of midnight and the staircase closed. The princesses were already in their beds, fast asleep.

The next night was the same. On the first stroke of midnight, the soldier followed the princesses down the staircase, and though he danced with the youngest princess in the castle by the lake for what seemed hours, when the princesses finally returned to their beds, the clock was just finished striking twelve. This time the soldier carried away one of the golden fruits from the garden.

And on the third night it was the same again, but when the soldier took the youngest princess's hand to dance with her, she sighed and looked into his eyes, and said, "I wish we could dance like this forever, but my father intends to find us out, and one day he will succeed. Then he will give one of us to the man who betrays our secret. But how could a man like that be a worthy husband?"

When the princesses ran to the boats, the soldier plucked a single sparkling flower, and followed them sadly to the lake, returning to their bedroom as always just as the clock struck the last note of twelve.

The next morning, the king called the soldier and the princesses to the throne room, and demanded whether the soldier had discovered the answer to the mystery.

The soldier looked at the youngest princess, with whom he had fallen in love. "Your majesty," said the soldier, "I know the princesses' secret, but I fear it is not mine to tell." And he laid before the princess the silver leaf, the golden fruit, and the flower bright as diamonds.

Then the youngest princess recognized her prince and dancing partner. "Do not kill him, papa!" she cried. "I will tell you the answer."

The princess told the king the whole story of the garden and the slippers, and in this way the enchantment was broken. The soldier and the youngest princess were married very happily, and the princess wore on her finger a sparkling ring like a flower.

RUMPELSTILTSKIN

ONCE UPON A TIME THERE WAS A MILLER WHO WAS
not very bright. He had a pretty daughter and decided he would go to the king
and try to get her a job in the king's castle. But when the king asked the miller
what his daughter could do, the miller was so awed by the castle and so flus-
tered by the king that he said the first thing that came into his head, which
happened to be a tremendous lie. The miller told the king that his daughter
could spin straw into gold.

"That is an extraordinary talent," the king said, frowning. "I suppose you
know that anyone who lies to me is put to death?"

"Yes, majesty," replied the miller miserably. So the miller's daughter was
brought to the castle, and the king shut her in a room with a spinning wheel
and a very large pile of straw and locked the door up tight.

"Check on her in the morning," he told his guards. "If the room is still full
of straw, bring her father to me."

The poor girl found herself in a terrible situation. If she did not spin the
straw into gold, her father would be killed for lying to the king. She burst
into tears.

Suddenly there was a little man before her, and he looked around at all the straw and said to her, "You are the girl whose father says you can spin straw into gold, I suppose. Why are you weeping?"

"Because I don't know how," she said hopelessly, wondering where this man came from and how he knew who she was.

"What will you give me," he asked, "to help you?"

"Anything you like!" exclaimed the girl.

"Well, then give me your necklace," said the little man, and immediately he sat down at the spinning wheel and began to spin.

As the first morning light crept into the sky, the little man got up from the wheel, turned around three times, and vanished. All the straw had been spun into gold.

The king, when he saw this, was impressed, but still skeptical. Was it some trick? "Do it again," he told the girl, and locked her up very carefully in a new room with a spinning wheel and an even larger pile of straw.

No sooner was the door closed than the little man appeared before her. "What will you give me this time to help you?" he demanded.

"Anything you like!" replied the girl again.

"Well, then give me your ring," said the little man, and sat down again at the spinning wheel and began to spin.

And again, as soon as it was dawn, he got up, turned around three times, and vanished, leaving all the straw neatly spun into gold.

The king was very impressed this time. He thought that a girl with such a talent might make a fine queen, but he wanted to be really sure that he was not being fooled. "Do it again," he commanded, and locked her in the deepest, safest room in his castle with a spinning wheel and an even larger pile of straw than before.

As soon as the door closed, the little man appeared again. "What will you give me this time to help you?" he asked.

"Anything you like!" said the girl, very glad to see him.

"Well, then give me your firstborn child," he said, and sat down to spin.

"What?" gasped the girl. "I can't give you that!"

"Then what about your father?" asked the little man. "The king will kill him."

Of course he was right, so the girl reluctantly promised him her first-born child.

When dawn came again, all the straw was spun into gold, and the little man had vanished once more. The king was very, very impressed, and very pleased. He let the girl know that he had decided to marry her and make her queen. All in all, this seemed a much better conclusion to her than her father being killed, so she married the king and lived quite happily with him for some time.

But over time she forgot her promise to the little man, and eventually gave birth to a beautiful baby boy. The nurse laid the child in his mother's arms, and right beside the queen, a voice said, "Hello."

There was the little man, and the queen looked at him in horror. "You promised me your firstborn child," the little man reminded her. But the queen fell on her knees and begged and pleaded for her child until the little man put his hands over his ears and said, "Enough! I will give you a chance, then. If you can guess my name in three days' time, you can keep your child. But if you can't, he's mine!" And the little man disappeared as quickly as he had come.

The queen went to her husband and told him the whole story, and while the king was angry at being fooled, he loved his wife and child, and did not want them hurt. So the king and queen spent the day thinking of all the names they had ever heard of, and the next morning, when the little man appeared, they guessed dozens of names, but the little man just shook his head. "Try again!" he cried.

So the king and queen spent the next day gathering names from everyone in the castle, and when the morning came again, they guessed hundreds of names. But the little man just shook his head. "Try again!" he laughed.

On the third day, the king and queen sent messengers out to all the country around them, to find the most unusual names anyone had ever heard of. The messengers returned with many very strange names, but the last messenger returned with a story.

"As I was coming back through the forest," the messenger told the king and queen, "I saw a light flickering in the trees. I followed it to a campfire, and there I saw an odd little man dancing around the fire and singing to himself. He sang,

> *"I'm smarter than the wind that blows*
> *and I'll win at every game,*
> *for no one guesses, no one knows*
> *that Rumpelstiltskin is my name!"*

The next morning, the little man came again.

"Is your name Cowribs? Or Spindleshanks? Or Spiderlegs?" asked the queen.

"No, no!" sang the little man in glee.

"Then is your name *Rumpelstiltskin?*" she asked.

The little man stopped dead, gave a great cry of rage, and stamped his foot, opening a deep crack in the earth. There he teetered on the edge for a moment, and then he fell into the crack, and fell, and fell, until he had disappeared in the darkness, and he was never heard from again.

THE BREMENTOWN MUSICIANS

ONCE UPON A TIME THERE WAS A DONKEY WHO WAS tired of carrying grain. "I have a very fine bray," thought the donkey. "I will go to Brementown and be a singer in the street."

So he set off, and on the road he met a dog, who was tired of guarding his master's house. "Where are you going?" asked the dog.

"I am going to Brementown, to sing in the street," replied the donkey.

"I have a very fine bark," said the dog. "I will go with you."

So the donkey and the dog set off down the road. Along the way they met a cat, who was tired of chasing mice. "Where are you going?" asked the cat.

"We are going to Brementown, to sing in the street," they replied.

"I have a very fine yowl," said the cat. "I will go with you."

So the donkey and the dog and the cat set off down the road. And on the road they met a rooster, who was tired of looking after the chickens. "Where are you going?" asked the rooster.

"We are going to Brementown, to sing in the street," they replied.

"I have a very fine cock-a-doodle-doo," said the rooster. "I will go with you."

So the donkey and the dog and the cat and the rooster set off down the road. Eventually evening fell, and, hungry and tired, they followed a faint light a little way into the forest. There they found a lonely cottage where a gang of robbers lived, and the donkey, who was tallest, peeked in the window.

"What do you see?" the others asked.

127

"Lots to eat and drink and a warm fire," replied the donkey. "But there are four robbers in there as well." So the four animals thought for a bit, and came up with a plan. The dog climbed onto the donkey's back, and the cat climbed up on top of the dog, and the rooster flew up and stood on the cat. And then, braying and barking and yowling and crowing, they leaped through the window with a tremendous crash. The robbers were so alarmed at this sudden attack that they fled from the house, though none were sure what had just happened. They met again in the forest and decided to wait until things were quiet to go back.

Meanwhile, the donkey, the dog, the cat, and the rooster made themselves at home, ate their fill, and turned out the light, sure that they'd driven off the

four robbers. Each animal settled down where it suited him best: the donkey lay down in the garden, and the dog lay down behind the door; the cat settled down by the embers in the hearth, and the rooster perched in the rafters.

When the light in the cottage had gone out and all had been quiet for some time, the robbers crept back to their house, and came in the back door. It was pitch black in the house, so one robber went to the hearth, and seeing the cat's eyes in the dark, thought they were embers, and tried to light a match at one of them. The cat leaped at the robber, yowling and scratching, and immediately the dog began barking, the donkey began braying, and the rooster crowed as loudly as he could. The robber screamed and tumbled into the other robbers, who all tried to get out of the house at once. One ran to the front door, where the dog bit his leg, and another went out the garden window, where the donkey gave him a solid kick, and the last struggled through the back door, with the rooster on his head.

Once they had escaped, the robbers found each other again in the woods, and discussed what had happened.

"I'm certain there's a witch in the house," said the first one. "She tried to scratch my eyes out!"

"And there's an enormous wolf by the door," said the second. "He nearly bit my leg off!"

"There's an ogre sleeping in the garden," said the third. "He hit me so hard with his club, it almost broke me in two!"

"And there must be a banshee as well," said the fourth. "Did you ever hear such an awful din?"

Finally the robbers decided that, as their house was clearly cursed, they would have to go somewhere else and make a new home.

But the donkey, the dog, the cat, and the rooster were so pleased with their new home that they decided not to go to Brementown at all. They became good friends and often sang together, and they all agreed the music was very fine.

THE FISHERMAN
AND HIS WIFE

NCE UPON A TIME A FISHERMAN LIVED CONTENTEDLY
with his wife in a little hut near the sea. Every day he woke early and went to
throw his line into the water.

One day, after angling for a long time without a single bite, the line suddenly went taut, and when he pulled it up again there was a large flounder
hanging at the end of it.

"Do not eat me!" exclaimed the fish. "Good fisherman, let me go; I am not
a real fish, but an enchanted prince. I shall be of no use to you, for I am not
good to eat. Put me back again into the water, and let me swim away."

"Ah," said the man, "you need not make yourself anxious. I would rather let a flounder who can speak swim away than keep it."

With these words, he placed the fish back in the water, and it sank away out of sight. Then the fisherman went home to his wife.

"Husband," said the wife, "have you caught anything today?"

"I caught a flounder," he replied, "who said he was an enchanted prince; so I threw him back into the water and let him swim away."

"Did you not make a wish?" she asked.

"No," he said, "what would I wish for?"

"Why, at least for a better hut than this dirty place. How unlucky you did not think of it! He would have promised you whatever you asked for. Go and call him now; perhaps he will answer you still."

The husband did not like this task at all; he thought it was nonsense. However, to please his wife, he went and stood by the sea. When he saw how

green and dark it looked, he felt much discouraged, but made up a rhyme and said:

> *"Flounder, flounder, in the sea,*
>
> *Come, I pray, and talk to me."*

The fish came swimming up to the surface, and said, "What do you want with me?"

"Ah," said the man, "I caught you and let you go today, without wishing; and my wife says I ought to have wished, for she cannot live any longer in such a miserable hut as ours, and she wants a better one."

"Go home," said the fish. "Your wife has all she wants."

So the husband went home, and there was his wife, no longer in her dirty hut, but sitting at the door of a neat little cottage, looking very happy.

She took her husband by the hand and said, "Come in, and see how much better it is than the old hut."

So he followed her in and found a beautiful parlor with a bright stove in it, a soft bed in the bedroom, and a kitchen full of earthenware and copper vessels for cooking. Outside was a little farmyard, with hens and chickens running about, and, beyond, a garden containing plenty of fruits and vegetables.

"See," said the wife, "is it not delightful?"

"Ah, yes," replied her husband, "as long as it seems new you will be quite contented; but after that we shall see."

"Yes, we shall see," said the wife.

A fortnight passed, and the husband was quite happy, till one day his wife startled him by saying, "Husband, after all, this is only a cottage, much too small for us, and the yard and the garden cover very little ground. If the fish is really a prince in disguise, he could very well give us a larger house. I should like, above all things, to live in a large castle built of stone. Go to your fish, and ask him to build us a castle."

"Ah, wife," he said, "this cottage is good enough for us; what do we want with a castle?"

"Go along," she replied, "the flounder will surely give us what you ask."

"No, wife," said he. "The fish gave us the cottage, but if I ask again he may be angry."

"Never mind," she replied, "he can do what I wish easily, and I have no doubt he will; so go and try."

The husband rose to go with a heavy heart, and when he reached the shore the sea was quite black, and the waves rushed so furiously over the rocks that he was terrified, but again he said,

> *"Flounder, flounder, in the sea,*
>
> *Come, I pray, and talk to me."*

"Now then, what do you want?" said the fish, lifting his head above the water.

"Oh dear!" said the fisherman, in a frightened tone. "My wife wants to live in a great stone castle."

"Go home," was the reply. "Your wife has all she wants."

The husband hastened home, and where the cottage had been there stood a great stone castle, and his wife tripped down the steps, saying, "Come with me, and I will show you what a beautiful dwelling we have now."

So she took him by the hand and led him into the castle, through halls of marble, while numbers of servants stood ready to usher them through folding doors into rooms where the walls were hung with tapestries, and the furniture was of silk and gold. From these they went into other rooms equally elegant, where crystal mirrors hung on the walls, and the chairs and tables were of rosewood and marble. The soft carpets piled the floors, and rich ornaments were arranged about all the rooms.

Outside the castle was a large courtyard, in which were stables and cow-sheds, horses and carriages, all of the most expensive kind. Beyond this was a beautiful garden, full of rare flowers and delicious fruit, and several acres of field and park land, in which deer, oxen, and sheep were grazing—all, indeed, that the heart could wish was here.

"Well," said the wife, "is not this beautiful?"

"Yes," replied her husband, "and you will think so as long as your mood lasts, and then, I suppose, you will want something more."

"We must think about that," she replied, and then they went to bed.

Not many mornings after this, the fisherman's wife rose early. It was just daybreak, and she stood looking out over the beautiful country that lay before her. Her husband did not stir, and presently she exclaimed, "Get up, husband, and come to the window! Look here, ought you not to be king of all this land? Then I should be queen. Go tell the fish I want you to be king."

"Ah, wife," he replied, "I don't want to be king. I can't go and ask that."

"Well," she replied, "if you don't wish to be king, I wish to be queen, so go and tell the fish what I say."

The husband went down to the shore in a sorrowful mood. A dreadful storm had arisen, and he could scarcely stand on his feet. But still he called up the fish with the old song, and told him his wife's wish.

> *"Flounder, flounder, in the sea,*
>
> *Come, I pray, and talk to me."*

"What!" cried the fish, rising to the surface, "She is still not content? Go home," said the fish. "Your wife has all she deserves."

He went home, to find all the glories and the riches vanished, and his wife sitting in the old hut, alone.

RAPUNZEL

ONCE UPON A TIME THERE WAS A WOMAN WHO looked into her neighbor's garden and coveted the fresh greens growing there. The garden belonged to an enchantress, and even in the dead of winter, it flourished with ripe vegetables and herbs in flower.

The woman loved above all other foods a particular green called rapunzel, and as the winter drew on and all the food to be had at market was either dried or bottled, the woman grew more and more envious of the enchantress's garden.

Finally she went to her husband and said, "I cannot go another day without green things to eat! Sneak into the enchantress's garden when the night is darkest, and bring me back some of her rapunzel!"

The husband did not like to do this, as everyone was afraid of the enchantress, but his wife gave him no peace, until at last, on a night with no moon, he climbed over the garden wall and pulled up a handful of rapunzel.

"Trespasser!" shrieked a voice. "How dare you rob my garden?" It was the enchantress, and her face was black with rage. The man begged her to have mercy, but the enchantress would not listen. She cast a spell over the man that twisted him into a juniper tree, and then she planted him in the spot where he'd pulled up her rapunzel.

When the woman's husband did not return, and she saw the juniper tree hunched in the enchantress' garden where the rapunzel had grown, she feared the worst, and went to the enchantress to beg for her husband's life.

The enchantress looked down at the woman with cold eyes. "How will I guard my garden against thieves if I do not punish those I catch?" she said. "If I return your husband to you, then you must give me in return no less than your firstborn child."

The woman, in her despair, agreed, and the witch changed the juniper tree back into the man, and husband and wife went home again very sad indeed.

In time, the woman had a child: a daughter with hair as bright as the sunlight. But no sooner had the child been placed in her mother's arms than the enchantress appeared at the door and demanded the baby for her own. As soon as the infant was in her arms, the enchantress disappeared, and no one saw her again.

The enchantress abandoned her house and garden, and traveled deep, deep into the forest. Where she stopped, she built a cottage, and raised the girl there, all alone.

She named the baby Rapunzel and soon came to prize her above all things. But as Rapunzel grew into a young woman, and her beauty shone brighter and brighter with each year, the witch began to fear that Rapunzel would leave her. So she built a tall ivory tower without a single door, but only a narrow window at the top, and she shut Rapunzel up there, and promised her a horrible punishment if she ever tried to escape.

When the witch wanted to enter the tower, she called up to the window, "Rapunzel! Let down your hair!" And Rapunzel, who had never had her hair cut, let down a long, long braid that the witch would climb up on.

But one day a young man came riding through the forest. He heard the witch call to Rapunzel, saw Rapunzel lean out the window, and he fell in love with her in a moment. So he waited for the witch to go away again, and when she had gone, he went to the foot of the tower and called out, "Rapunzel! Let down your hair!"

Rapunzel thought it was the witch calling, so she was shocked when the young man climbed in at her window instead. She had never seen any other

person besides the witch, and she marveled at the stranger who now stood in her room. But the young man spoke to her kindly and told her of the wide world that she had never known, so when he asked her to come away with him, she answered, "Yes."

So with his sword they cut her hair, and tying it to the window, climbed down the braid. They quickly hid themselves in the forest, for just then the witch returned. Seeing Rapunzel's golden hair already hanging out the window, she became angry and called out, "What are you doing, wicked girl? Just wait till I get up there!"

But when the witch climbed to the top, the young man gave the braided hair a great yank and pulled it down, trapping the witch in her own tower.

The witch screamed curses at them from the window, but they rode away, and not long after they were married very happily. They built a cozy house, and around it they planted a verdant garden, where all were welcome.

ACKNOWLEDGMENTS

We wish to thank the following properties, whose cooperation has made this unique collection possible. All care has been taken to trace ownership of these selections and to make a full acknowledgment. If any errors or omissions have occurred, they will be corrected in subsequent editions, provided notification is sent to the compiler.

Front Cover	Honor C. Appleton, from *A Treasury of Tales for Little Folks*, 1927.
Endpapers	Gustave Dore, from *Contes du Perrault*, 1862.
Half-Title	Arthur Rackham, from *The Fairy Tales of the Brothers Grimm*, 1909.
Half-Title Spot	Margaret Tarrant, from *Favourite Fairy Tales*, n.d.
Title Page	O. Kubel, German postcard, n.d.
Title Page Spot	Jeannie Harbour, from *My Book of Favourite Tales*, n.d.
Copyright	Arthur Rackham, from *Cinderella*, 1919.
Preface	Ludwig Emil Grimm, drawing of his older brothers, n.d.
Contents	Florence Harrison, from *Repunzal*, 1914.
12	M. S. J., stone lithograph of Cinderella, circa 1890.
14	Charles Folkard, from *Grimm's Fairy Tales*, 1911.
15	Anonymous, from *My Nursery Tale Book*, n.d.
16	W. H. Margetson, from *The Old Fairy Tales*, n.d.
17	Jeannie Harbour, from *My Book of Favourite Tales*, n.d.
18	W. Gunston, from *Cinderella*, 1876.
19	Millicent Sowerby, from *Cinderella*, n.d.
20	Maxfield Parrish, *Cinderella (Enchantment)*, 1913.
21	Anonymous, from *The Nursery Picture Book*, n.d.
22	O. Offerdinger, from *Marchenbuch*, n.d.
23	Anonymous, from *The Nursery Picture Book*, n.d.
24	Anonymous, from *Stories Children Love*, 1927.
25	Jeannie Harbour, from *My Book of Favourite Tales*, n.d.
26	Elenore Abbott, from *Grimm's Fairy Tales*, 1921.
27	Margaret Evans Price, from *Once Upon a Time*, 1921.
28	Edmund Dulac, from *The Sleeping Beauty and Other Fairy Tales*, n.d.

29   Lancelot Speed, from *The Red Fairy Book*, 1890.

30   Honor C. Appleton, from *A Treasury of Tales for Little Folks*, 1927.

31   Anonymous, from *The Ideal Fairy Book*, n.d.

32   Anonymous, from *The Nursery Picture Book*, n.d.

33   Anonymous, from *Past Pleasures*, circa 1880.

34   Sir John Everett Millais, *The Woodsman's Daughter*, 1851.

35   Al Bowley, from *Old Fairy Tales*, n.d.

36   Margaret Evans Price, from *Hansel and Gretel*, n.d.

37   R. Andre, from *Grimm's Household Fairy Tales*, 1890.

38   Kay Nielsen, from *Hansel and Gretel*, 1925.

39   "Phiz" (Hablot K. Brown), from *Grimm's Goblins*, 1861.

40   Al Bowley, from *Old Fairy Tales*, n.d.

41   Nora Fry, from *A Treasury of Tales for Little Folks*, 1927.

42   Arthur Rackham, from *The Fairy Tales of the Brothers Grimm*, 1909.

43   John R. Neil, from *The John R. Neil Fairy Tale Book*, n.d.

44   John Hassall, from *Blackie's Popular Nursery Stories*, n.d.

45   Paula Ebner, from *Gebruder Grimm Marchen*, 1924.

46   Herm Vogel, from *Kinder- und Hausmärchen*, 1894.

47   Herm Vogel, from *Kinder- und Hausmärchen*, 1894.

48   Herm Vogel, from *Kinder- und Hausmärchen*, 1894.

49   Herm Vogel, from *Kinder- und Hausmärchen*, 1894.

50   Herm Vogel, from *Kinder- und Hausmärchen*, 1894.

51   Herm Vogel, from *Kinder- und Hausmärchen*, 1894.

52   Bess Livings, from *Snow White and the Seven Dwarfs*, n.d.

54   W. H. Margetson, from *The Old Fairy Tales*, n.d.

55   Anonymous, from *My Nursery Tale Book*, n.d.

56   O. Kubel, German postcard, n.d.

57   Anonymous, from *My Nursery Tale Book*, n.d.

58   W. C. Drupsteen, from *Snowdrop*, n.d.

59   John Hassall, from *Blackie's Popular Nursery Stories*, n.d.

60   Paul Menerheim, from *Kinder- und Hausmärchen*, 1885.

61   Bess Livings, from *Snow White and the Seven Dwarfs*, n.d.

62   Walter Crane, from *Household Stories*, 1886.

63   Arthur Rackham, from *The Fairy Tales of the Brothers Grimm*, 1909.

64   Kay Nielsen, from *Hansel and Gretel*, 1925.

65   Anonymous, ephemera, n.d.

66   O. Offerdinger, from *Marchenbuch*, n.d.

67   Bess Livings, from *Snow White and the Seven Dwarfs*, n.d.

68   A. B. Frost, from *Phantasmagoria*, 1919.

70   W. H. Margetson, from *Stories of Grimm*, n.d.

71   W. H. Margetson, from *Stories of Grimm*, n.d.

72   Walter Crane, from *Grimm's Fairy Tales*, 1884.

74   N. M. B., from *The Old Fairy Tales*, n.d.

75   Jessie Willcox Smith, from *A Child's Book of Stories*, 1919.

76   Anonymous, from *Little Red Riding Hood*, circa 1900.

78   Jeannie Harbour, from *My Book of Favourite Tales*, n.d.

79   Millicent Sowerby, from *Grimm's Fairy Tales*, 1909.

80   Gustave Dore, from *Contes du Perrault*, 1862.

81   W. Tomlinson, from *Grandmama Goodsoul's Edition*, 1880.

82   Margaret Tarrant, from *Favourite Fairy Tales*, n.d.

84   Edmund Dulac, from *The Sleeping Beauty and Other Fairy Tales*, n.d.

85	Anne Anderson, from *The Sleeping Beauty*, n.d.
86	Edmund Dulac, from *The Sleeping Beauty and Other Fairy Tales*, n.d.
87	Millicent Sowerby, from *Grimm's Fairy Tales*, 1909.
88	W. Heath Robinson, from *Old Time Stories*, 1921.
89	Anonymous, from *The Ideal Fairy Book*, n.d.
90	Anonymous, from *The Favourite Book of Nursery Tales*, 1893.
91	Charles Folkard, from *Grimm's Fairy Tales*, 1911.
92	Anonymous, from *The Favourite Book of Nursery Tales*, 1893.
93	Warwick Goble, from *The Fairy Book*, 1913.
94	Anonymous, from *My Nursery Tale*, n.d.
95	Arthur Rackham, from *The Arthur Rackham Fairy Book*, n.d.
96	Walter Crane, from *Household Stories from the Brothers Grimm*, 1886.
97	Francis Kirn, from *The Annual Mammoth Book*, 1946.
98	Francis Kirn, from *The Annual Mammoth Book*, 1946.
99	Charles Folkard, from *Grimm's Fairy Tales*, 1911.
100	Anonymous, from *The Brave Little Tailor*, n.d.
102	Francis Kirn, from *The Annual Mammoth Book*, 1946.
103	G. Uplaud, from *Collected Tales of the Brothers Grimm*, n.d.
105	H.J. Ford, from *The Blue Fairy Book*, 1890.
106	Walter Crane, from *Household Stories from the Brothers Grimm*, 1886.
107	E. H. Wehnert, from *Household Stories Collected by the Brothers Grimm*, 1853.
109	H.J. Ford, from *The Red Fairy Book*, 1890.
110	Arthur Rackham, from *The Fairy Tales of the Brothers Grimm*, 1900.
111	Claude Aubriet, from *Elements de Botanique*, 1694.
112	Kay Nielsen, from *In Powder and Crinoline*, 1913.
113	Anonymous, scrap art, n.d.
114	Al Bowley, from *Old Fairy Tales*, n.d.
116	Charles Folkard, from *Grimm's Fairy Tales*, 1911.
117	Anonymous, from *Routledcge's Coloured Picture Book*, 1870.
118	Margaret Evans Price, from *Once Upon a Time*, 1921.
119	George R. Halken, from *Rumpelstiltskin*, 1882.
120	R. Gunther, from *Tales of Grimm*, n.d.
121	George R. Halken, from *Rumpelstiltskin*, 1882.
122	Al Bowley, from *Old Fairy Tales*, n.d.
123	Warwick Goble, from *The Fairy Book*, 1913.
124	Noel Pocock, from *Grimm's Fairy Tales*, 1913.
125	Al Bowley, from *Old Fairy Tales*, n.d.
126	John Hassall, from *Popular Nursery Stories*, 1940.
128	Corinne Malvern, from *Storytime Tales,* circa 1948.
129	Harry Rountree, from *Told to the Children*, 1936.
131	Josef Scharl, from *Grimm's Fairy Tales*, 1944.
132	Kay Nielsen, from *Hansel and Gretel*, 1925.
133	A. J. H., from *Grimm's Fairy Tales*, 1909.
134	A. J. H., from *Grimm's Fairy Tales*, 1909.
137	Wanda Gag, from *Tales From Grimm*, 1936.
138	Anonymous, from *Rapunzal*, 1909.
141	Anne Anderson, from *Grimm's Fairy Tales*, n.d.
142	Walter Crane, from *Household Stories from the Brothers Grimm*, 1886.
Back Cover	Anonymous, from *My Nursery Tale*, n.d.